MW01128188

# SUMMER STORM

## A Satan's Fury MC Romance Series

## L Wilder

Copyright © 2015 L Wilder
Print Edition

All rights reserved. Without limiting the rights under copyright reserved above, no part of this publication or any part of this series may be reproduced without the prior written permission of both the copyright owner and the above publisher of this book.

This book is a work of fiction. Some of the places named in the book are actual places found in Paris, TN. The names, characters, brands, and incidents are either the product of the author's imagination or are used fictitiously. The author acknowledges the trademarked status and owners of various products and locations referenced in this work of fiction, which have been used without permission. The publication or use of these trademarks is not author-ized, associated with, or sponsored by the trademark owners.

This e-book is licensed for your personal enjoyment only. This e-book may not be re-sold or given away to other people. Warning: This book is intended for readers 18 years or older due to bad language, violence, and explicit sex scenes.

Cover by: Carrie at
https://cheekycovers.com/

Warning: This book is intended for readers 18 years or older due to bad language, violence, and explicit sex scenes

# MAVERICK

There are things that happen in our lives that mark us forever. That change us in ways that we don't even understand. One chance meeting and fate casts her irrevocable spell. They say what doesn't kill you only makes you stronger, and that God doesn't give you more than you can handle. Unfortunately, those are just words, and they don't change shit.

I thought I had a good life, one I could be proud to call my own. My club meant the world to me, and I was proud to have them as my family. I knew I could depend on my brothers, and honestly they were really all I'd ever needed.... until I met Hailey. She was beautiful, smart, and sexy as hell. The woman captivated me.... Then she ripped my beating heart from my chest.

The hurt she caused cut me to the core. Her web of lies had had a catastrophic effect on my life and everyone else's she had come in contact with, but she wasn't around to see it. She wasn't around to see how her choices had affected so many people. No... she was gone. Gone from all of our lives forever, leaving me and mine and everyone that loved her in her wake, picking up the pieces of her betrayal.

This is my brother Guardrail's story. As VP, he was the one chosen to rectify the damage Hailey and her deceit had caused the club. He thought it would be simple – find the culprits and deal with them accordingly. He wasn't prepared for the storm that ensued… none of us were.

## Chapter 1

# ALLISON

"PARKER, ANY LEADS on a contractor yet?" My boss asked gruffly as he leaned against the doorway of my office.

I jumped in surprise, torn from my wayward thoughts and flustered by the sudden unwelcome intrusion.

"I have several I'm looking into now, actually," I replied with feigned confidence. It wasn't entirely true; I had really only focused on one.

"Well... let's get a move on it. The plans should've been finalized weeks ago," he said with a heavy sigh. I could tell he was guarding his words to hide his frustration. Normally it drove me nuts when Neil micromanaged me, but this time even I had to admit he had good reason. He had finally agreed to let me take the lead on a major project, and I had lost my focus. It was so unlike me. I normally got totally lost in my assignments. It was always so liberating. I loved putting my all into a worthy cause, and I had finally gotten the perfect opportunity to do just that.

"I need to have a full proposal with your chosen contractor by the end of the week," he asserted. He was done being polite, and I knew I'd be in hot water if it wasn't done on time.

"It will be ready, Mr. Yates. You know I wouldn't let the kids down."

"I know. I know. I'm just ready to get things started. Thanks for everything you do, Ms. Parker," he said as he walked out of my office. My mind started reeling as reality set in. The project was my chance to make a real difference. I needed to stop acting like a foolish teenager and pull my shit together. I couldn't afford to screw it up.

I knew firsthand how difficult being raised in the foster system could be. After my parents died when I was six, my older brother and I were put into foster care. Unfortunately, we were separated, and our foster families couldn't have been more different. Tony was placed with a family that already included four other foster kids, and their backgrounds were nothing like ours. He was surrounded by troubled teens and rebellion during his most formative years. Sadly, it became difficult for us to keep in contact as the turmoil took its toll and engulfed his home life.

My foster life wasn't filled with chaos and anarchy, though. Mine was... lonely. I was placed with a kind couple named Tom and Wendy who hadn't been able to have children of their own. They were nice, but not nice enough to take on my brother. In the beginning, after relentless pleading, they let him visit on several occasions, giving me vague hopes we could be reunited. When that didn't happen, I pulled away from their love. I didn't want a new family. I had a family, and I wanted them back.

I wasn't willing to just give up on being with my brother. He was too important to me. Through the years, I'd done everything in my power to keep in touch with him, but things changed and he started pulling away. He was always keeping secrets from me, and it worried me. I could see the angst in his eyes, but he wouldn't talk about it. When I asked him why he was pushing me away, he told me it was for my own protection. I tried to understand why he was doing it, but it still hurt. There was nothing I could do to help him, but there was no way I was going to lose him completely. Even if I didn't get to see him very often, I made sure to keep in touch through emails and phone calls, reminding him every chance I got that I would always be there for him.

Being without him, I retreated into myself and spent most of my time alone growing up. It wasn't until I started visiting the local community center that I finally started coming out of my shell. I met some of the other foster kids in town, and we created our very own sanctuary there. We would meet to hang out and play basketball or talk through things if we were in a tough spot. It was a place where we felt safe. We didn't feel judged or inadequate. We weren't outsiders there. We belonged.

That community center helped me learn how to deal with my anger and pain and turn it into something positive. Watching the older kids mentor the younger children helped me realize what I wanted to do with my life. I'd been working with the foster care system for the past eight years, and I'd devoted my life to making things better for those kids. Ever since I could remember, I'd wanted to find a way to make a difference, and I thought building a Youth Center would be a great way to help. I knew how much the community center where I had grown up had affected me, and it was important to me to make sure that these local kids had that support, too.

The center had to provide a stimulating environment for kids of all ages. I knew it needed to have a wide range of programs, activities, camps, and special events for the kids throughout the year. They needed to have a place to feel safe and spend time with their friends. It had taken a lot of work and fundraising, but I'd finally gotten it approved. Our Downtown Youth Center would have classrooms, a fitness center, a large auditorium, and a gymnasium with basketball courts. We would be able to offer activities and classes for the kids and their foster parents. I'd worked hard to make this project a possibility, and I wanted it to be perfect.

Once I had completed all the details, I placed several ads with all of our specs and projected budget. I encouraged any contractors that might be interested to contact me about submitting their bids, and the inquiries quickly began to fill my inbox. After reading through several offers, one in particular caught my attention. I wasn't sure what made his email stand out, but something pulled me to ask him for more information.

He and I spent the next few hours emailing back and forth. At first, the emails primarily consisted of contractor inquires and references, but then they grew increasingly more personal. I even found myself wondering if he was flirting with me a little. He was charming and funny, and I admit, I loved the attention. My imagination ran wild with possibilities of what the rugged, charismatic construction worker might have looked like. With every email, my mind tried to piece together my fantasy man. Our little online routine progressed just like that for several days. I still continued to look into the other offers, but his remained at the top of my list. After all, he had great references, and his proposal was below the budget. And… okay, there was something about seeing his name in my inbox that always made my heart skip a beat. I just couldn't resist.

I had gotten completely wrapped up in the fantasy, and I just didn't know what I was thinking. The Youth Center had been my dream for so long, but suddenly the charming stranger had taken over my every thought. He was like a drug, each message leaving me craving more. I found myself compulsively checking my inbox, looking for my fix. He had me hooked. Over the next week, the number of messages increased as the conversations became more addictive. I knew I should've stopped messaging him. He was a potential employee, and no good could come from it. But I couldn't stop myself. The truth was… I didn't want to.

It was easy to get lost in the fascination of some mysterious man, but it was more than that. I felt like I was getting to know him through his emails. His interest… his hobbies… even what he wanted in the future. This Kane Blackwood was no simple man. He was passionate about his work, and he was proud of the success he'd had at SF Construction. Kane was not afraid of hard work. It was one of the things I found most endearing about him. When he told me that he was a member of a motorcycle club, I was immediately intrigued. There was something about that secret world that I found appealing. As crazy as it sounded, the idea of having a group of brothers that had your back, of having a family that you could always turn to, made me envy him. When he first mentioned his motorcycle, I found myself fantasizing about what it would be like to ride with him. I had never been on one before, but the thought of it excited me, giving me goosebumps all over. Everything about him excited me, and truthfully, that scared me a little. The more we talked the more he seemed to be genuinely interested in me. That made me feel... well... wanted.

Honestly, the whole thing was the ideal situation for me. I'd always kept men at an arm's length, even if I really liked them. It was an unfortunate side effect from my solitary childhood. I didn't let my guard down easily, so romantic relationships had always been a struggle. My little online infatuation was the perfect mix of intimacy and self-preservation. I got the affection I craved without the danger of having to be truly vulnerable. The anonymity of being online gave me the safety net I needed to be confident and flirty... brazen even. I allowed myself to open up for the first time in forever and engage in a little harmless fun. He had a way with words, and it was hot. I didn't want it to end.

We continued down that path for almost two weeks, messaging back and forth every chance we got. As Neil started to remind me of our deadlines, though, I began to get nervous. I was going to have to actually meet Kane soon and get the ball rolling on the Youth Center. No more hiding behind my computer. I had to show him the location of the building site, and I needed to discuss the blueprints with him.

Neil had started prowling around just outside of my office, glancing in my direction like he knew something was going on. I shook my head and tried to focus on the task at hand. I pulled up my email, and after explaining Neil's demands, I asked Kane if he could meet me at the site on Thursday. I had to get things started and fast. Time was up. As soon as I hit send, my heart started to race. What if I had been wrong about everything? What if he was some kind of serial killer? Or a fat, balding old man with a boner for younger women? I had been so stupid, but there was no turning back. I had no plan B. When his response popped up on my computer screen, however, all my doubts quickly disappeared.

**May 1, 2015**
**2:45 p.m.**
**Kane Blackwood**
**SF Construction**

**Morning All-Star,**

**So Thursday's my lucky day, huh? Just tell me where and when, and I'm in. Don't**

**worry about your presentation. I'll make sure I'm ready; you just make sure *you're* ready. I'm going to need you all day to get this done right.**

BUTTERFLIES AND FEAR raced through me as I read his words. I smiled to myself when I saw the new nickname he had for me. I still don't know what had possessed me to tell him that silly story. I'd nearly died of embarrassment the day I tried my hand at baseball. I never forgot the expression on the coach's face as my ball crashed through the front windshield of his car. He was furious. It didn't matter that I had actually hit the ball for the first time; he was too busy freaking out about his car. I never was able to hit the ball like that again, and eventually I gave it up altogether. Sports were just not my thing.

## Chapter 2

# GUARDRAIL

**"H**OW'S OUR LITTLE project going? Have you found out anything we can use?" Maverick asked.

"I know she isn't frightened of the club life like she should be, if that's any indication of how much she talks to her brother," I told him as I took a drink of my beer.

"You think she has any idea what he's been up to?" he asked.

"No. Nothing has come up on any of the feeds. He hasn't been to her house, and there hasn't been any communication between them through her phone or email. The prospects are still rotating shifts, and none of them have seen any sign of him."

As Vice President of Satan's Fury, it was up to me to find Tony, the lowlife motherfucker that stole a fifty thousand dollar shipment from the club. Because he'd been a long-standing leader of one of the street gangs in town, he'd gotten a unanimous vote at the table for the drug distribution. He was a professional, but in the end, he'd decided he could fuck us on our money. Surprisingly, the asshole actually thought he'd be able to get away with it.

He'd forgotten that Satan's Fury owned the whole damn town. Because drugs were an unavoidable reality in the outer east and west side of our territory, we negotiated which gangs could run product and where. It was the best way for us to keep control of what drugs were sold in our area. We'd allowed Tony and his minions to distribute our product, same as the other little set on the west side. We used them out of necessity. Our product kept us in control of the territory. They did the distribution, and we took our cut… a large cut.

Nobody in the clubhouse talked to anyone about anything, so we were caught off guard when Tony managed to manipulate Maverick's girl, Hailey, to get information about the club. It cut deep. Maverick had it bad for Hailey, and no matter how many times she'd come and gone, he was always there for her. Hell, he didn't even realize she'd gotten hooked on junk until it got bad, and even after that it took an overdose for him to finally be able to cut her off. Although we all knew he would never share club business, the whole situation had us all on edge.

The last time she called Maverick begging for money, he'd tried putting her off by telling her he was going on a run and wouldn't be back for a week. Unfortunately, Hailey's decision to give Tony that little tidbit of information had given him a five-day jump that nobody saw coming, and it had cost us... big. We'd come home early only to find that Tony and his crew had taken off with our money, and Hailey was nowhere to be found. It was a shit ton of fuckery.

They had to be found... all of them. We knew Tony was hiding, and we had eyes everywhere. It was only a matter of time before we found him. We started with their families. Unfortunately, none of them kept any strong family ties that we could pull intel from. They had kids like kittens, and too many baby's mamas to count. Since we decided that cutting the head off the snake was our best option, Maverick, our Sergeant of Arms, and I have spent weeks searching for information on Tony's whereabouts. When we came across the name of his sister, we both agreed she was our best lead.

"Has she said anything about Tony? Do you think she knows where he is?" Maverick asked.

"Nothing yet, but she's opening up more every day. If she does know anything or he contacts her, I'll get her to talk," I told him confidently. I could tell she was beginning to trust me. A part of me felt guilty about misleading her, but in the end, I knew I didn't have a choice.

"You'll find him. Once you put your mind to something, there's no stopping you," Maverick told me as his hand slapped against my back. "That's why the Pres put you on this."

"I'll do whatever it takes to find him, and he'll pay for fucking with the club," I told him as I slammed my empty beer bottle down on the counter. "He will slip up, and I'll be there waiting when he does."

From what I could tell, Allie hadn't spent a lot of time with her brother recently. They'd both been in the foster care system, but growing up in separate homes had made them completely different people. She'd made a life for herself, while Tony fell deep into drugs, alcohol, and gang life. I'd been able to retrieve several emails he'd sent her over the past few years. It was obvious that Tony did what he could to keep his sister from his lifestyle, but whenever he got down on his luck, she was always the first one he'd reach out to. She always remained loyal to him. Even when she knew his life was spinning out of control, she was there when he tried to contact her. Her love for her brother never wavered, and I respected her for that.

He'd royally fucked up this time, and something in my gut told me that he'd try to contact her. Just like he always had, he'd come running to her when the shit hit the fan. I needed to get in contact with her, so when I saw the ad in the paper, I knew I had my in. I'd known that she worked for Child Services, but I didn't realize that she was so invested in making things better for those kids. I had to admit, I liked that about her. It was one thing to work with them every day, but this was more than an ordinary house visit. This would help a lot of kids all at once, and she'd come up with the entire plan herself.

"If she knows something, you'll get it out of her," Maverick told me with confidence. "Just be patient."

"Yeah, but it may be harder than I thought."

"Why's that?"

"It's… I don't know, man. She's just not what I expected," I confessed. "Hell, I don't know how to explain it."

"I get it, brother. I've seen her picture. She's a hot ass. I can see why you might get a little distracted," he snickered.

"It's not that. She's just… different," I told him. "I thought she'd be some kind of stuck up bitch. Hell, you've seen her… all dressed up in that fancy shit, business suits and high heels. I wasn't expecting her to be so… whatever. It doesn't matter. If she knows something about Tony, I'll get it out of her."

"Ha, wait a minute… sounds like she's getting to you, brother," Maverick prodded.

"Maybe, but it's just a job. Finding out where that dickhead ran off to is my only focus," I told him, but I knew it wasn't that easy. I was a selfish bastard, and I wanted it all. Ultimately, I knew I had to deal with Tony, but Allie definitely had me thinking. I found myself in an impossible situation, and I had no idea if I could make it work.

"Whatever you say, man. Just be careful with all that. Remember, her brother is walking dead... nothing is going to change that. If you need any help, you know where to find me," Maverick offered.

Maverick was a good man, one you could depend on. Unfortunately, he had a hard time believing that. He was still carrying around a lot of guilt from the shit that'd gone down over the past few months, but he never let that get in the way of the club. He was a brother that you could always depend on.

"Thanks, man," I responded.

"Hey, you never know... maybe this thing with her will work out. I've seen crazier things happen."

"Good things like her don't happen to me, brother," I told him, shaking my head. He patted my back as he turned to leave. As I watched him walk out of the bar, my mind drifted back to Allie. I found myself wondering if Maverick could be right. Was there a way that I could actually have her? Without thinking, I pulled out my phone to see if she had responded to my last email. I couldn't stop the smile that spread across my face when I saw her name.

**May 1, 2015**
**3:15**
**Allison Parker**
**Department of Children's Services**

**All-Star?? Really? You're going to pay for that one, mister. :)**

**Looking forward to Thursday. I'll bring the coffee.**

THE GIRL WAS getting to me. I knew that she was becoming a real distraction, and I needed to focus on her lowlife brother. There was one problem though… I couldn't stop my finger from hitting the reply button.

**May 1, 2015**
**3:30**
**Kane Blackwood**
**SF Construction**

**I'll take mine however you like yours, All-Star.**

**See you Thursday.**

**May 1, 2015**
**4:25**
**Allison Parker**
**Department of Children's Services**

How do you do that? You give me a crazy nickname, and I'm sitting here smiling like a goof. I think you're getting to me.

BTW, thanks for the "coffee order." :)

## Chapter 3

# ALLIE

W HEN I WALKED into the office, everyone was standing around grumbling as they drank their morning cup of coffee. I smiled and tried not to act too eager about getting back to my office. I wanted to check my email. I hadn't been online since yesterday afternoon, and I was curious to see if Kane had messaged me back.

As soon as I sat down at my desk, I saw that I had a message in my inbox. I anxiously clicked the button to open my emails, and his name was the first one that caught my attention.

**May 2, 2015**
**9:45 p.m.**
**Kane Blackwood**
**SF Construction**
**Like that I'm getting to you, babe.**
**Night.**

**May 3, 2015**

**9:08 a.m.**

**Allison Parker**

**Department of Children's Services**

**Morning, :)**

**Hope you're having a good day. I've been thinking about you. Wondering if you're as good with your hands as you say you are....**

JUST AS I was about to click the send button, Neil walked into my office, interrupting my train of thought. "Daniel sent over the changes to the blueprints this morning. Have you had a chance to look them over?"

"I was just about to ask you about that. Do we really have to take out the meeting room?" I asked with a sad sigh.

"Allie, it's just not in the budget. If you can find a way to fund it, then you can have him put it back in the plan," Neil said as he leaned against my doorframe. His arms were crossed and resting on his protruding belly. I had to fight the urge to roll my eyes at him.

"Maybe we could reduce the size of the fitness center," I suggested.

"We've already made that deal with Health and Fitness Retro. We can't risk losing their sponsorship."

"You're right. I just hate to see things get taken away. We've worked so hard. I want everything to be perfect."

"Focus on finalizing the bids. I want to have it on my desk by Friday afternoon. I need to check everything over before the board sees it on Monday," Neil told me.

"I'm meeting the contractor on Thursday."

"Be ready to present any new ideas to them on Monday. They're eager to hear what you've been working on."

"I'll have everything ready," I promised.

He nodded and stepped into the hall. "Looking forward to it," he called back.

I turned back to my computer and started to gather my files.

**May 3, 2015**
**12:25 p.m.**
**Kane Blackwood**
**SF Construction**

**Are you questioning my abilities, All-Star?**

**May 3, 2015**
**1:10 p.m.**
**Allison Parker**
**Department of Children's Services**

**I know better than that.**

**May 3, 2015**

**1:15 p.m.**

**Allison Parker**

**Department of Children's Services**

**Anyway, Mr. Confident,**

**I am actually looking forward to seeing you live up to this reputation of yours. :)**

**May 3, 2015**

**1:35 p.m.**

**Kane Blackwood**

**SF Construction**

**Ms. Curiosity,**

**I will. Don't you worry about that, sweet-heart.**

I WAS TRYING to think of a flirty response to Kane's last email when a text message from my brother popped up on my phone. My heart dropped. I hadn't heard from him in weeks and seeing a phone number I didn't recognize really made me start to worry. There had to be something wrong. There was a time that I'd thought Tony was the best brother in the world. I'd looked up to him and thought he would always be there to protect me. In his defense, I think he tried. I knew a part of him worried about me, but his life had taken a different turn than mine. He didn't want me involved in the things he was dealing with, so he pulled away from me... only sending text messages or emails to keep in touch. I hated it. He was the only family I had left, and he chose drugs and money over me. It hurt.

**Need to talk to you. It's important.**

**T**

WELL, SHIT. THAT didn't sound good. I had to wonder if he was in some kind of trouble. The last time we talked, I could tell that he was upset about something. He wouldn't tell me what was going on, but I could see the concern in his eyes. I didn't think twice about confirming that I would be there. He was the only family I had left. I had to help him if he needed it.

## Chapter 4

# GUARDRAIL

"**N**EED TO KNOW where we are with To-ny," Cotton told me. As club president, he ruled with an iron fist. When he gave an order, he expected results... immediate results, and I had nothing. He was depending on me to deal with Tony, and I could tell he was getting restless.

"Meeting the sister today," I told him asser-tively. "I've got this, Pres."

"We've got to make an example of him, Kane. No one fucks with the club... no one." The deep crow's feet around his dark eyes crin-kled as anger crept over his face.

"He'll slip up, and when he does, I'll be there. You can count on that," I told him, trying to reassure him.

He tugged thoughtfully at the ends of his long white goatee as he said, "What about this Youth Center? You really going to try for that with everything that's going on?"

When Cotton came up with the club starting its own construction company, I was intrigued. He wanted a cover for the money we were bringing in from early distribution, and we both agreed that a company like this would be the perfect front. I had no idea if we'd be able to pull it off, but I wanted to give it a try. I'd always had a passion for building things, and I was good at it. At first, we built small houses, trying to build a name for ourselves. It didn't take long for us to become one of the best companies in the city. Our work was good, and we submitted the best bids to ensure our growth. Everyone came to us, and we were constantly expanding. It truly was a perfect cover. Not only did it launder money for the club, it provided all the patches working there viable proof of income as well.

"It's one of the biggest projects we've had in a while. If they accept the bid, it could be a real good opportunity for us… opening doors down the road," I told him.

"I get that, but this whole thing could get messy. It's not about getting the job. She could find out that you're looking for her brother, and that would have consequences. Just play it safe," he ordered.

I nodded and walked out of his office. There was no point in arguing with him. I knew he was right. This wasn't about some fucking construction project. It was about finding Tony. I had to make myself remember that.

I headed down the hallway to my room. I wanted to get changed before I met up with Allie. I threw on a pair of jeans and a plaid button-down shirt, trying to play the part of the contractor she would be expecting. Before I left, I went by the office to pick up everything I might need for my meeting with her. I wanted to get to the site early, so I could look over things one last time to check my figures. I knew it was crazy, but I wanted to get the bid for my own selfish reasons. I'd pretty much left her fucked with no time for other options, and truthfully, now I wanted more time with her regardless of if it got us Tony.

I was leaning against my truck when she pulled into the parking lot. I patiently waited as she fumbled around inside the car. Then, she finally opened the door and stepped out. As soon as her high heels hit the pavement, my eyes followed the line of her long, slender legs up to her thighs where her skirt had hiked up a little during her drive. The curls of her long, brown hair flowed down around her shoulders, concealing her face as she looked down to adjust her short, gray skirt. Damn. That sexy ass skirt hugged her curves in all the right places, bringing my cock to life right in the fucking parking lot. She quickly pulled her hair to the side and looked over to me. Her beautiful, pouty lips slowly curved into a sexy smile as her dark brown eyes met with mine. At that moment, all my thoughts of Tony were instantly forgotten. He became a distant memory as my entire mind was devoured by the beauty standing before me.

"Hey there, handsome," she said. Just the sound of her voice made the world stop turning on its axis. I couldn't explain it. It was like she had cast a spell on me, and I was unable to resist it. I wanted her. Hell, just seeing her standing there made me think about the future. I'm not that kind of man... I had never thought about my future... not with anyone, but now suddenly I was envisioning bike rides, a white picket fence... even rugrats running around. It didn't make any fucking sense. I watched as she started walking towards me, her hips casually swaying from side to side. Her gorgeous smile never wavered as she approached me. Perfect... she was fucking perfect.

"Looking good, All-Star." A light blush of red crossed her cheeks as she tucked her hair behind her ear. Beautiful.

"Always the charmer," she said as she handed me a cup of coffee. "You definitely know how to make a girl smile."

"I can think of more than a few ways I'd like to bring a smile to that beautiful face," I told her and grinned as I saw the curiosity flicker in her eyes. I stepped closer, and her breath stopped, only confirming what I already knew. She was into me. The sexual energy was raging between us immediately. I fucking loved it.

"You're quite the flirt, Mr. Blackwood."

I leaned down, just inches from her ear, and whispered, "Just stating the facts, sweetheart." She shifted her feet and awkwardly fumbled with the lid on her coffee cup. I loved watching her try to hide her body's reaction to me, but it was useless. I could tell that I was getting to her. "And call me Kane."

"Okay… Kane," she said with a bashful smile, looking down at her coffee cup.

"Don't get shy on me now, darling," I told her as I inched closer to her. We had shared so much over the past few weeks in our messages, I felt like I truly knew her.

She tilted her head as she looked up to me with wonder. She slowly lifted her hand up to my face and placed the palm of her hand on my cheek. "Are you really here? Is this really happening?"

"Yeah, Allie. It is," I told her.

"I thought I had made it all up in my head," she said with a light chuckle.

"Allie."

"I was worried that you might be some kind of creeper."

"No one said that I wasn't," I said, laughing.

"Or bald."

I couldn't hold back my laugh, "No... I'm not bald."

"I can't believe it. I never thought I could get to know someone... to have feelings for someone without actually meeting them first. I feel like...."

"I know, Allie. I know exactly what you mean." I leaned down and pressed my lips against hers, immediately feeling my body come alive in a way it never had before. Her touch set me on fire. The intensity was almost too much, but I couldn't pull away. I needed more. My hands reached for her hips, pulling her body into mine as she opened her mouth to me... warm and wet. Fuck. She was every man's fantasy... my fantasy. Mine. A light moan vibrated through her chest, urging me on as I deepened the kiss, claiming her mouth with mine. Her fingers tangled in my hair, forcing a growl to escape through my lips. I wanted her... all of her. A thousand thoughts raced through my mind as I stood there holding her close to me.

She was everything... everything I could never have. Suddenly, my heart felt like it was clamped in a vise. What the fuck was I thinking? Our club was going to kill her brother. He was the only family she had left, and we were going to take him from her. Damn. I knew better than this. I knew she'd never be able to forgive me.

We were destined to be destroyed. I pulled back and looked down at her. Her lips were full, damn near bruised from our kiss and begging to be kissed again. I took a deep breath and did my best to rein in my need for her. I couldn't let it happen. Not then... not like that.

"Kane?" she asked. Her face was marked with confusion as she looked up at me. "Is something wrong?"

"No, Allie," I told her as I stepped away from her. As hard as it was, I knew that I had to stop. I couldn't lead her to believe that there could be something between us, when I knew what the end would be. I didn't want to hurt her, but there wasn't any way around it. "We... um, we just need to talk about the specs."

"I.... Sure. I wasn't thinking," she said as she took a step back.

"I've already had my guys survey the area, so I just need to know if there have been any changes since we talked last night," I told her, trying to sound professional.

"No, everything is all set. Neil wants to review the final quote before we present it to the board on Monday. Do you think you could give it to me by tomorrow?" she asked nervously.

"Allie...do you trust me?" Her face filled with anxiety, and it gutted me. "I'll have it. I told you not to worry. I've already done most of the work. I'm pretty close to wrapping it up."

"Really? Are you sure?" she asked excitedly.

"I'm sure. I'll send it over to you tonight," I told her. She was just about to say something else when her phone rang. She reached into her side pocket and pulled out her phone. I could see the worry in her eyes the moment that she read the message. Her hands trembled as she stared at her phone.

"Allie? What is it? What's wrong?" I asked.

"It's nothing. It's just my brother. He needs to see me about something," she said, sounding a little nervous.

"You look upset. Are you okay?" I asked as I reached out and ran my hand down her quivering arm, trying to comfort her.

"Yeah… yeah, I'm fine. He just wants to meet up," she said as she fiddled with the buttons on her phone.

"When? Do you need to leave now?"

"No, no. We're meeting at Lancaster's on Sunday at 7:00," she said with a heavy sigh. "I'm just worried that he's gotten himself into some kind of trouble again," she mumbled, thinking out loud.

"Don't worry about it. It's not a big deal. Everything will be fine," she continued, but I could see the apprehension in her eyes. I didn't like it… not one damn bit. I'd known he would contact her, but as much as we needed to find him, I'd hoped that he wouldn't pull her into his shit. There was no reason for him to put her in danger. I couldn't believe that son of a bitch was planning on dragging her to that dump Lancaster's, but now that he was, I would do whatever it took to keep her safe.

## Chapter 5

# ALLIE

M Y DRIVE HOME was a total blur. My mind was spinning, reeling from that kiss... that unexpected, perfect kiss. I brought the tips of my fingers to my mouth and smiled as I touched my swollen lips. I could still feel the sensation of his mouth against mine. I'd never been kissed like that before, and it had left me longing for more. But he'd stopped, and I just couldn't understand why. There was obviously something bothering him, and I had to think that it was me. Maybe I had misread everything. I thought back to all of our conversations, and up until he pulled away, I had really thought he was interested in me. I knew I wasn't imagining the sexual chemistry I felt when we kissed. Damn. I really liked him, and I'd thought he felt the same way about me. I couldn't help but feel a little disappointed that I might have been wrong.

When I thought about it, I realized that Kane

looked nothing like the men I had dated in the past. His dark hair was pulled back in a ponytail, and he had several cryptic tattoos trailing down his arm. In any other situation, I would have thought his large build and huge biceps were intimidating, but all I could do was fantasize about being wrapped in his arms. I found him to be incredibly attractive, and as I'd walked towards him, I could feel my entire body physically reacting to him with every single step I took. The man had enchanted me with his bluish gray eyes that pierced straight through to my heart. With just one look, I felt him claim me in every way I could ever imagine.

From the very beginning, I'd known things were going to be different with him. Until now, I'd never really had the desire to get to know the men I was dating on a deeper level. It seemed too intimate. It was just safer to keep my walls up and play along with them and whatever made them happy. I guarded my heart and kept them at a distance. It wasn't like that with Kane, though. I wanted to get to know him, and until that kiss, I thought he felt the same way about me. Now I was confused. The look on his face left me doubting everything, and I didn't know what to think anymore.

Instead of going back to work, I decided to drive straight home. I needed to decompress. I wanted a long hot bath and a strong drink. After

I'd soaked in the tub for almost an hour, my mind was still reeling from everything that had happened throughout the day. I desperately needed to escape for a bit. I decided to put on my favorite shorts and t-shirt and search for a good, funny movie. I needed a good laugh, so I settled on *Crazy, Stupid, Love.* Unfortunately, just as Ryan Gosling threw Steve Carrell's 407s over the rail, my phone chimed with a new message from Tony.

**I can't wait til Sunday. Need to see you now. Lancaster's – 30 minutes**

**T**

His timing sucked, but there was no way I could tell him no. I replied back, telling him that I would be there and quickly began to change my clothes. As I made my way up to Lancaster's, I couldn't help but wonder what was going on with him this time. I knew something had to be horribly wrong, or he wouldn't have been so eager to see me. All of the worst-case scenarios ran through my head. The fear for his wellbeing consumed me.

I tried to prepare myself for what lay ahead, but as I walked into the rundown, almost condemned, bar my anxiety only intensified. The whole place gave me the creeps. All of the customers seemed shady and from the rough side of town. The lights were dim, and the cigarette smoke made it difficult to even see. With burning eyes, I made my way to the back of the bar where Tony was waiting for me.

When I approached, he barked, "It's about time you got here."

"Tony, I got here as fast as I could. I'm not even late." His knees were bouncing under the table, and I could tell that he was on edge. I'd never seen him look so upset. "What's going on with you?" I asked. "Is something wrong?"

"Sit down, sis," he said firmly.

"That bad, huh?" I asked as I threw my purse down in the booth and sat down. I watched as he glanced around the room like he was expecting someone to jump out and get him. He was obviously freaked out, and it was starting to scare me.

"I need your help, Allie. And I need it now. I've run out of time," he said desperately.

"Why? What's going on, Tony? Just tell me. Be honest!"

"I need money, Allie. Serious money, and I need it now," he said as he glanced around the bar yet again, making sure no one was watching us. "You gotta give me twenty-five thousand dollars... now."

"Twenty-five thousand dollars! Are you insane?" I shouted.

"I know you've got savings. It's not like you've got kids or family or anything. I am your family. Can't you get an emergency loan against your condo? It's only twenty-five thousand dollars... you could even get your bank to give you a signature loan for a car in twenty-four hours. Why don't you try that? They'll hand you a check. If I don't get it soon, they're going to kill me. You have to help me, sis. Please," he pleaded.

"Tony, seriously... there's no way I can get my hands on that kind of money," I told him. "I want to help, Tony. I love you. You know I do. You're my brother. I just don't know if it's possible for me to get that much money."

"What about the Youth Center? Didn't you rake in all kinds of money with all those fundraisers and shit?" he snapped.

"Are you kidding me? Are you really asking me to steal?" I asked, completely stunned. "You know I can't do that!"

I was in shock. I couldn't believe that he even considered asking me to do something like that. He knew how I felt about my job, about helping those kids. There was no way I would ever do anything to jeopardize my career.

"Allie... they're going to kill me! Hell, they'll probably come after you, too, if I don't get them this money. These guys don't fuck around. They will come after us. I promise you that."

"Who? What have you done? What have you gotten yourself into? Why would they come after me? How do they even know about me? You hide your whole life from me. I don't even know any of the people you associate with. You're scaring me, Tony," I told him. I tried to fight back my tears, but there was no use. The thought of someone hurting him made my chest ache. I couldn't even process the fact that I had been drawn into his mess. All I could feel was my heart pounding, each beat striking harder than the last. What was I going to do? He was the only family I had left, and I couldn't lose him.

"You should be scared, sis. Hell, I'm scared. I'm scared to death. I've gotta get this money fast, or we're dead," he stressed.

I was completely overwhelmed, but I knew I had no other choice. I had to try and help him. "I'll see what I can do," I told him.

"Thank you, Allie. You're my last hope," he said as he reached over and squeezed my hand.

"Can't promise you anything, Tony," I told him. "I have no idea if I can pull this thing off, but I'll do everything I can. You can't expect me to steal from my work, though. That's not an option, but I'll do what I can. I love you. You're not alone in this," I promised. "I'll contact you as soon as I know something."

He quickly stood up and towered over me, his eyes glowing in urgency. "You have to, Allie. You have to!" He slammed his fist against the table, causing everyone in the bar to look in our direction. When he saw them looking, he lowered his voice to a strained whisper and said, "I've gotta get out of here. I'll be in touch… and Allie?"

"Yeah?"

"Hurry!" he pleaded before he turned and walked out of the bar.

Shit…. it was so much worse than I thought.

## Chapter 6

# GUARDRAIL

A S SOON AS I left Allie, I headed straight to the clubhouse. I had to get to Big Mike. After hearing that Tony had contacted Allie, it was on. Even though she told me he didn't plan to meet up with her until Sunday, I wasn't leaving this in the prospects' hands. Tony was desperate and could turn up at any time. I wanted to know the minute he showed up, and Big Mike was the best man for the job. In addition to being one of the bigger guys in the club, he was also our best hacker. He could get into any computer system in just a matter of seconds, so I knew he wouldn't have any trouble getting into her phone messages. Luckily, he wasn't hard to find. After pounding on his door, I walked into his room and found him hacking away at his computer.

"Hey, Big Mike. Tony contacted Allie. It's time to move on this. I need you to hack into her phone and monitor all of her calls and texts from this point on."

"You got it, brother. I'm on it," he reassured me. "I've got this." He patted me on the shoulder. "You don't have to worry about me monitoring it. Here's a shadow phone. I'll have it up and running in less than an hour. You'll be able to monitor her yourself directly. It will automatically ring when hers does. Every phone call or message she gets will come through this phone as she gets it, instantaneously. You can answer, and she won't even know you're listening."

"Perfect. Let me know if anything else comes up," I told him.

"Will do," Big Mike nodded. "I'll check every angle and go through the numbers that Tony used to contact her and see if we can get a lead from them, too," he said.

"Good. I need a beer. I'll check back in thirty," I told him as I left his room and headed to the bar.

I needed a minute to clear my head and was relieved to find that the bar was fairly empty. Most of the brothers were still at work, so it was quiet. Cassidy was behind the counter and smiled when she saw me walking in her direction. There was a time when I would've been interested in that smile. Not anymore.

"Hey there, Guardrail. Want a beer? Or something stronger?" she asked.

"Just a beer. Give me my usual," I told her as I sat down.

"You look like you have something on your mind, hun. You want to talk about it?" she asked. Of all the sweet butts, she was the only one with an actual heart. I wouldn't have wasted my time on most of the club girls around there. They were only interested in getting their hands on a property patch, and you can't make a hooker a housewife. Cassidy was different, though. She seemed to really care about the club, and I liked that about her.

"Always got something on my mind, Cass. Today isn't any different," I told her as I took the beer from her hand. That wasn't exactly true. I'd never had my every thought wrapped up in a woman like this before, and I could feel the tightness growing in my chest when I thought about something happening to her.

"Well, I'm here if you want to talk about it," she offered.

"Thanks. Just want to drink my beer."

"Let me know if you change your mind," she said as she turned and headed over to finish cleaning the bar top.

I'd just finished off my beer when Big Mike stormed up to me with an anxious look on his face. "Tony made contact about thirty minutes ago. He's meeting her at Lancaster's right now."

"Fuck!" I shouted.

"Want me to head over there?" he asked.

"We'll both go… and get a few of the others to come along. If he's still there, we don't want to risk him getting away," I ordered. "And tell the prospects to stay at her place. I want to know when she gets back."

"I'll meet you out front in five minutes," Big Mike told me.

True to his word, five minutes later Big Mike met me out front with three brothers and four prospects. We headed straight for Lancaster's, but by the time we got there, Tony was gone. There was no sign of anyone. When I described Allie and Tony to the bartender, he said that we'd only missed them by a few minutes.

"Want me to head over to her place?" Big Mike asked.

"I'll go. Be on call. If something comes up, I need you to be ready," I told him.

"You know I will," he told me as he followed me out to my bike. "You think Tony will turn up there?"

"No idea, but I'll be there in case he does," I told him as I started up the engine. He nodded and turned to leave as I pulled out of the lot. I needed to get to Allie. I had to find out if she was okay. The thought of something happening to her was killing me. Fuck. The woman had her hands wrapped around my heart. I was a goner, and there wasn't a damn thing I could do about it.

Usually riding calms me down, but there was an eerie stillness to the night that had me on edge. I knew in my gut that something wasn't right. Just as I turned into Allie's neighborhood, my three prospects whipped past me. They were chasing several of Tony's crew, which meant they'd spotted them near her house. Fuck. I could feel my pulse racing through my veins as I imagined what could have happened if they hadn't been there. In a matter of seconds, I was off my bike and pounding on her front door.

## Chapter 7

# ALLIE

"KANE?" I ASKED. He was the last person I expected to see, and I didn't know what to make of the intense look he had on his face. "Uh, what... what are you doing here? And how do you know where I live? What's going on?"

"Nothing. Nothing... I, uh, I just needed to see you," he said in a rush, trying to sound nonchalant and failing miserably. He stood there staring at me, relief clearly flooding his face. I could tell he was holding something back, but I was in such shock, I didn't even care. I had to will myself not to reach out and touch him and prove to myself that he was really there. As thrilled as I was, though, I was equally baffled by the expression on his face. I had no idea what to think, but I was glad that he was there... whatever his reasons were. I had been on edge since my conversation with Tony, and there was something about seeing Kane's face that made me feel safe.

"You want to come in for a drink or something?" I offered.

"Sure. You got a beer?" he responded as he walked into the room and closed the door behind him.

"Yeah, let me go grab us one. Just make yourself comfortable," I said before turning towards the kitchen.

When I returned, he was sitting on the sofa, his eyes glued to me as I walked over and handed him the cold beer.

"Is everything okay, Kane?" I asked again as I sat down beside him.

He looked over to me and said, "Yeah… everything's fine now."

"Well, good. I guess," I replied with a confused nod. "So, do you want to watch a movie or something?" I asked.

"I could watch something," he said with a slight smile. I was relieved to see him start to relax.

I picked up the remote and started flipping through the movie channels, trying to find something I thought he might like. I got flustered because I had no idea what to pick, so I finally gave up and handed it over to him. "Here, see if you can find something."

He scrolled through several channels before stopping on some old thriller I'd seen several times before but couldn't remember the name of. "Is this the one where the boyfriend goes nuts and tries to kill her family?" I asked.

"No idea, but it has Mark Wahlberg in it, so it can't be all bad."

As we watched the movie, I nervously fiddled with the label on my beer bottle. The butterflies in my stomach went wild every time I looked over in his direction. I still wasn't sure what had brought him over, and I was feeling a little insecure.

"I'm glad you're here. It's a nice surprise. I've, umm… I've been thinking about you," I confessed.

"Is that right? And what exactly have you been thinking about me?" he asked with his eyebrow cocked high.

Color rushed to my cheeks as his attention turned to me. "Just… you know, it was nice getting to meet you after all of our messages. I was relieved that you weren't some psycho just trying to get into my pants."

"No one said I wasn't trying to get into your pants, All-Star."

"Oh, really?" I asked playfully. I was teasing, but a part of me was curious to see what he would do.

"Yeah… really," he whispered. A thrill shot through me, and I couldn't stop the mischievous grin that spread across my face.

He brought his hands up and rested his palms against my cheeks, slowly brushing his calloused thumb across my skin. He looked at me for what seemed like an eternity. Damn. There was something about him that made my body tremble with need, and having his body so close to mine was enough to send me over the edge. I watched in wonder as he lowered his perfect mouth down to mine, kissing me softly… so gentle and sweet. His scent circled around me, a mix of cologne and fresh leather. Just being close to him enthralled all of my senses.

I couldn't resist him, even if I wanted to. His pull was too strong… I was falling for him, and there wasn't a damn thing I could do to stop it. As soon as I brought my hands up to his chest, the kiss changed, becoming more intense and heated. Goosebumps swept across my flesh as he delved further into my mouth, exploring every inch with his tongue. His fingers dug into my hips as he pulled me closer to him, forcing a light moan to vibrate through my chest. The bristles of his beard lightly scratched against my skin as he took complete control of the kiss. My body ached for him, burning for more as he claimed me with his mouth. My hands began to roam over his chest, gliding over the bulging muscles of his abdomen. I wanted to touch his bare skin, feel the heat of his body pressed against mine. I couldn't wait any longer. Without thinking, I began to tug at his vest, pulling it from his body. He took it from me, carefully setting it over the back of the couch. Once he turned back to me, I reached for the hem of his t-shirt and pulled it over his head. Once it was off, our hands became frantic, quickly removing the clothes that separated us. In just a few seconds, I was wearing only my lace bra and panties. My lips curved into a smile as I looked over to his clothes thrown haphazardly on the floor along with my pink satin bathrobe and nightie.

"Kane?" I whispered. I couldn't stop staring at him. My eyes traveled along the lines and curves of the muscles of his chest, marveling at all of the tattoos that marked his body. I loved how he stared at my almost naked body with lust-filled eyes. I watched in eager fascination as his chest slowly rose and fell with each tortured breath he took. I could hear a faint growl escape him as his mouth settled over mine. We both sunk deeper into the cushions of the sofa as his hands slowly eased behind my back to release the clasp of my bra. As the fabric slipped away from my body, I felt his lips glide across my skin to my breast. Lust consumed me as the wet heat of his mouth engulfed my nipple and began to gently suck. He broke contact momentarily as he pulled back slightly and his strong arms repositioned me on the couch, his hard body moving to cover mine. His mouth resumed its heavenly torture of kissing and nipping the delicate skin of my neck. As he settled between my thighs, I rocked my hips, grinding against him as I tried desperately to find relief for the throbbing that was building up inside me.

"Steady, All-Star," he whispered in my ear. His hand slowly slid between our bodies as he said, "I'm just getting started."

He traced his fingers across my panties, teasing me with his light caresses. Pushing the fabric to the side, he slowly slid his finger into me. He twirled and flicked his fingers inside me, tormenting me with the motion of his hand.

"Is this what you want, baby?"

As I let my legs spread farther open for him, he growled, "That's it, baby. Give it to me."

His thumb circled around my swollen clit, drawing out my pleasure. As he found my g-spot, I held my breath, the muscles in my body quivering uncontrollably. I was still soaring in ecstasy when I felt my panties being ripped from my hips. The cushions underneath me shifted as he reached over for a brief moment to his clothes on the floor. I lifted my head just long enough to watch him slide the condom down his long, thick shaft. Then, a look of satisfaction crossed his face as he settled back between my legs and positioned his cock at my entrance.

"You ready for me, Allie?" he panted. "You want me?"

"God, yes!" I moaned.

He smiled appreciatively before his face took on a look of determination. He was struggling to control his lust that much was clear.

He clenched his jaw before lifting my hips and making one forceful thrust deep inside me, filling me completely. For a moment, I worried that I wouldn't be able to take much more, but he remained still until my body was able to accommodate his invasion.

"Mm, damn, you feel so fucking good," he growled. He slowly began to move, each thrust deliberate and powerful. I rocked against him with every stroke, trying to take him even deeper inside. His gaze burned into me as he brought his hand up to my neck, his fingers gently caressing my throat.

"This body is mine, Allie. All of you is mine, and I'm not letting you go." The intensity of our connection was there in his eyes, and there was no denying that I felt it, too. I had felt it from the moment we first spoke.

"Yes…please…" I groaned in pleasure, reassuring him that I felt the same way. I was lost in the waves of carnal sensation he was giving me, the fullness of his body inside mine. His eyes never left mine as he increased his rhythm, each thrust more demanding than the last. My inner muscles clenched around him as I felt another orgasm building inside me. "Oh, God! Don't stop!" I pleaded.

His punishing pace never faltered as his body continued to crash into mine. I'd never felt such an intense mixture of pleasure and pain. It was so intoxicating that I was finding it difficult to even breathe. His very touch sent me spiraling out of control, and I knew I would never be the same again. I wanted to remember everything about that moment... to focus on how incredible he felt, but it was all just too much. I couldn't stop my treacherous body from seeking its ultimate high. I let out a strangled moan as my orgasm took over, my body jerking beneath him. I wrapped my legs tighter around him as the jolt of my release drove him to find his climax. A sublime sense of satisfaction rushed over me as his growl echoed through the room. His body trembled and the muscles in his abdomen grew taut as he finally came deep inside me. Tremors of pleasure wracked his torso as he lowered his body down onto mine, pressing my breasts against his chest. He looked down at me reverently as our shallow breaths mingled in the air between us. I felt so close to him in that moment, I never wanted it to end.

His breathing began to steady as he slowly started to lift his body from mine. I wanted to wrap my arms around him and keep him close, but I hesitated. When he noticed my reaction, he paused to stroke my cheek and whispered, "I meant what I said. I'm not letting you go." Then, without another word, he stood and headed for the bathroom.

I was slipping on my bathrobe when he came back into the room. Without saying a word, he reached down, grabbing his clothes from the floor. A devious smile spread across my face as I watched him slide his jeans over his hips.

"Like what you see, All-Star?" he asked playfully.

"Hmm... yeah. You could say that," I said as I smiled and ran my fingers through my hair. This man definitely knew how to get to me. Trying to change the subject, I asked, "So... why did you really show up here tonight?"

"I just wanted to see you... make sure that you were okay," he told me, pulling his shirt down over his chest.

"Why wouldn't I be okay?" I asked.

"You looked worried earlier today when your brother called. Couldn't get it off my mind," he confessed.

"Yeah, well," I said as I tightened the belt of my bathrobe. "I was right about Tony. He's in some trouble."

"Did he say what kind of trouble?" he asked.

"He needs money... *a lot* of money," I replied with a heavy sigh.

"What kind of money are you talking about, Allie?" he asked with a mix of concern and anger in his voice.

"Twenty-five thousand dollars."

"And what exactly did he want *you* to do about it?"

"He asked me to get it for him, but I don't have that kind of money. I'll have to go to the bank and see if they'll give me a loan or something," I told him. Just the thought of the whole situation overwhelmed me. I could barely afford to pay my own bills. How was I ever going to be able to pay off that kind of debt?

"Have you really thought about this?" he asked as he crossed his arms over his chest.

"He's in trouble, Kane. I have to do something to try and help him. I've never seen him like this. He's seriously desperate. What kind of sister would I be if I didn't even try to help?"

"Allie, do you really think giving him this money is going to help him?"

"No idea, but he said these people were going to kill him if he didn't get it."

"Who says they aren't going to kill him either way? Can you really trust him?"

"I don't know… but he said they might even come after me!" Just saying those words sent chills down my spine.

"Fuck that. I'm not taking any chances with you, Allie. You're going to come stay with me."

"What?" I couldn't even comprehend what he was saying. My mind started running a mile a minute, and I couldn't think of a logical response.

"We'll sleep here tonight, but in the morning, we're going to my place," he demanded. "I'm not going to let anything happen to you."

"Kane… that's not necessary. Tony wouldn't let anything happen to me."

"If your brother had your safety in mind, he wouldn't have brought you into his mess. He should have protected you and left you out of it."

"But he needs me, Kane."

"Allie, your brother obviously has gotten himself into some serious trouble. I doubt there's enough money in the world to get him out of it. You have to trust me on this. He fucked up, and there's nothing you can do to help him. But know this… I will not let anything happen to you."

## Chapter 8

# GUARDRAIL

I WAS RELIEVED when Allie finally agreed that staying with me was the best option. She wasn't exactly happy about the idea, but I could tell that this thing with Tony seriously scared her. The motherfucker was up to something. He'd played the game long enough to know that just giving the money back wouldn't stop us from killing him. Once he betrayed the club like he did, he knew there was no way Cotton would let him walk away. There was another reason why he wanted that money from Allie, and I needed to find out what it was before she got hurt.

Later, as we laid in bed after another round of the best sex I'd ever had in my life, I looked down at her, all curled up next to me with her head resting on my shoulder and knew she was it for me. She was the one. I would give my life to protect her. She was mine now, and I wouldn't let him or anyone else fuck with her. Her fingers trailed along my arm as she continued to talk about all the different things that popped into her head, giggling from time to time when she remembered something funny. I loved hearing her laugh. She was exactly the way I had always imagined she would be when we were messaging back and forth. So full of life... filled with hope that everything would turn out the way it should. I admired that about her. I'd always been the kind of man that expected the worst, and I was rarely left disappointed.

"You think you could take me for a ride on your bike sometime?" she asked. "I've never had the chance to ride on one before."

"Maybe tomorrow."

"Really?" She said with a huge grin spreading across her face. "You know, I'm actually really looking forward to seeing your house tomorrow. It's going to be nice to see where you live."

"You're a curious one, aren't you, All-Star?"

"Maybe a little, but I wouldn't have to be so curious if you weren't so *mysterious*," she said with a laugh. "Sometimes I feel like you're trying to keep something from me."

"You'll know everything you need to know soon enough," I told her.

"See... so *mysterious*!" she said as she laughed again and nudged my side with her elbow.

"Allie, I'm not exactly a good guy. You should know this. I've lived a hard life... done some bad things, but I am loyal to those that I care about. I'll do whatever it takes to keep you safe and care for you like no other."

"You've already shown me that… about two hours ago," she said as she snickered. "And I like you just the way you are."

"Get some sleep, baby," I told her as I kissed her on her forehead. "You've got work tomorrow."

"Shit! I forgot about the…."

"It's done. I already emailed it to you."

"Kane… thank you so much. You don't know what that means to me."

"I wouldn't let you down, Allie. I know you've worked hard on this project. I'll make sure everything is done right."

"I trust you. I know it will be perfect," she told me.

"Sleep, Allie."

"Kane?"

"Yeah, baby?"

"I'm really glad I met you," she said in almost a whisper. "You're even better than I imagined that you would be."

"You're an amazing woman, Allison Parker. I'm going to spend my life reminding you of that every chance I get," I told her as I pressed my lips against hers. The kiss was brief, but filled with promise… my promise to her.

## Chapter 9

# ALLIE

I SPENT MY day at work in a complete daze. I was still trying to wrap my head around everything that had happened with Kane. I liked that he was so protective of me and wanted to make sure I was safe, but he couldn't stop me from trying to help Tony. He was my brother, and I had to see if I could do something to help him.

I pleaded with every bank in town, trying to get a damn loan, and every one of them turned me down... every single one. It was like they knew they were going to tell me no before I ever started talking. I just couldn't get them to budge. I was out of options, and I dreaded telling him that I couldn't come up with the money.

At least there was one positive thing... Neil seemed pleased with Kane's proposal. He was thrilled that it was below the budget, and he said he couldn't wait to show the board on Monday. I was relieved to have him off my back. Now I would be able to focus on other things....

Kane was waiting for me in my driveway when I got home. He was eager to get my things packed and over to his house. Once we got everything loaded into my car, I followed him over to his place. I was surprised when he pulled into the driveway of an old historical home with a Washington Heritage sign in the front yard. It was the kind of house you would see in *Better Homes and Gardens*, nothing like I had expected.

Once I put my car in park, I hopped out and walked over to him. "This place is unbelievable, Kane," I told him as I followed him up to the front door. "Is this really your house?"

"Yeah. I told you about it," he said, like it wasn't even a big deal.

"I'd say you downplayed it a bit. Don't ya think?"

"Maybe," he said with a big smile. "It's just a house, Allie."

"This," I said, "is not just a house!"

After we unpacked my car, he took me on a short tour, showing me all the renovations he'd made and told me about his plans for the rest of the house. I could see the pride in his eyes as he talked about it, and I couldn't believe he had done all of it on his own. It was amazing. There was much more to him than I had even realized.

When he finished showing me around, he turned to me and said, "Now that you're settled, we need to head over to the clubhouse. I've got some things I need to see about."

"Now?" I asked, feeling suddenly nervous about seeing the clubhouse for the first time.

"Yeah. I should've been there an hour ago."

"Okay. Give me a minute to change clothes," I told him as I turned and headed back to his bedroom. I quickly changed out of my work clothes and into a pair of shorts with a tank top and a pair of flip-flops. I looked in the mirror, giving myself one final check, before I headed out to find him.

He stared at me for a moment before he said, "You don't wear shorts on a bike, Allie. It isn't safe. Did you bring any jeans?"

"I get to ride on your bike?" I couldn't hide the excitement in my voice. I quickly headed back to change my clothes again. When I walked back into the room, he nodded in approval.

"Your legs looked hot in those shorts, All-Star. Best sight I've seen in awhile, but your ass looks amazing in those jeans, too," he said playfully. He didn't even give me a chance to react before he took hold of my hand, leading me out the front door and out to the driveway to his huge motorcycle. I didn't even realize they made them this big, but then again, it would have to be huge to carry a guy like him around. He threw his leg over the seat and held out his hand to help me get on behind him.

Once he was settled, he handed me a black helmet and said, "Put this on." After slipping it over my head, I used his shoulder for balance as I eased myself onto the bike. Without saying a word, he took my hands and wrapped them around his waist. The engine quickly came to life, and the vibrations of the motor shook throughout my body. He reversed out onto the main road and said, "Hold on tight."

My fingers locked around him like a clamp, securing me tightly to his back. I was completely wrapped around him. I couldn't have gotten any closer to him even if I'd tried. I was nervous, but the thrill of the ride excited me more. As he throttled back the accelerator and shot out into traffic, I realized I'd never felt anything more exhilarating. I was terrified and overjoyed all at the same time.

After several miles and a couple terrifying bends, I began to relax a little. I no longer had my hands fastened around him as tightly. I slowly slid them inside his leather jacket and rested the palms of my hands on his stomach, feeling his muscles tense as he controlled the powerful machine beneath us. I followed the rhythm of his body, leaning and swaying right along with him as we continued down the road.

Once I began to feel more comfortable, I started to actually look at the beautiful scenery that surrounded us. Dark threatening clouds began to roll across the sky, signaling an approaching storm. I knew it was about to get bad when sudden strikes of lightning flashed across the sky. Every time I saw a bolt of lightning strike the ground, I clamped my thighs tightly around him. The advancing storm should have worried me, but I felt so at ease next to Kane. Being with him made me feel safe and whole. As my nerves began to settle once again, my hands got a mind of their own. Every few minutes, they would find a new spot to rest on Kane's body… his thighs… his abdomen… his chest. Unable to stop myself, I began to shamelessly squeeze the inside of his thigh.

I could hear the hunger in his voice as he turned his head back towards me and said, "You're going to pay for that when we get to the clubhouse."

Losing all of my inhibitions, I let my hand drift farther up his thigh, lightly brushing my fingertips against his cock. I leaned forward, putting my mouth close to his ear and said, "Is that a promise?"

The bike slowed, almost to a stop, as Kane's voice took on a gravelly tone and said, "Behave, Allie."

I could feel my arousal growing as the vibrations of the engine rattled between my legs. I wanted him… right then and there. Brazenly, I again ran my hand more firmly over his hardening bulge and called, "Kane?"

"We're almost there," he growled.

As we made our way to the clubhouse, the rain suddenly broke free from the clouds. The storm was really setting in, and the tiny pellets of water had begun to sting against my skin as his bike tore down the road. Even with the lightning and pouring rain, my mind stayed focused on only one thought... Kane. I had never felt so much desire for a man, and I was having a hard time restraining myself. My hands roamed across his newly soaked shirt as I pressed my body against him.

"Allie," he warned as his hips shifted slightly in his seat. I knew I should have stopped. I knew it was already difficult for him to drive in the downpour, but I couldn't resist... I wanted him too much. Without warning, his bike veered from the road and down a grassy path toward an enormous oak tree. We skidded to a stop as the rain continued to pour down in sheets around us. He got off the bike and turned to face me, his eyes filled with intensity. "Off," he commanded. "Now."

## Chapter 10

# GUARDRAIL

I WATCHED AS she slowly took off her helmet, uncertainty etched in her eyes as she looked to me. Then, warily, she climbed off my bike and carefully placed the helmet back on the seat before turning toward me.

"Allie," I said firmly. She didn't reply. I could tell that I had caught her off guard with my tone. She stood quietly, staring at me apprehensively as she waited to be reprimanded.

"Allie, do you know how dangerous it was to be messing around on the bike like that?"

Still she didn't answer. Instead, her head lowered as she looked up at me through her lashes and gave a small nod. Her hands began nervously twisting the water from the bottom of her shirt. It was obvious she knew she'd crossed the line.

"Come here," I said firmly. Her eyes locked on mine in surprise, unsure of what to expect, but she didn't move.

"Kane, I'm sorry..." she began. "I just got carried away. I wasn't thinking...."

"Allie. Come. Here," I demanded again. Slowly, she began to move closer to me. With each step, I could feel the desire I'd restrained on the bike returning. Her hands' anxious squirming had pulled her soaking t-shirt tight against her perfect tits. As she approached, my eyes locked on her rigid nipples peeking through the thin fabric, and I felt the last bit of my self-control dissolve.

"Kane, I..." she started. Her words halted as I quickly closed the distance between us and took her in my arms. All uncertainty on her face immediately melted away and was replaced by a mischievous smile. "Oh," she finished as she bit her bottom lip seductively and looked up at me. Her eyes were full of expectation as they roamed down to my mouth. She licked her lips in anticipation and pressed her body harder against mine.

"Mmm, damn it, woman. What am I going to do with you?" I groaned as she brought her face up to mine.

I could feel her warm breath on my cheek as she whispered, "Oh, I can think of a few things." My hand slid up her wet shirt to the smooth skin of her neck as my lips found hers. Her sweet, full mouth pressed unrestrained against mine, matching my need, and begging me for more. A soft moan escaped her as my tongue swept across her lips, compelling them to open. My tongue surged into her mouth, winding with hers in a rush of passion that I couldn't refuse. My arms wrapped around her body and lifted her from the ground as I backed her against the massive oak tree. The rain that had been coming in cascades was slowed by the branches. Water trickled down through the leaves and fell upon her body. I continued to kiss and nip along her neck, tasting the mingled flavors of her salty, sweet skin and the cool rain.

Her eyes fixated on me as I began to remove my wet clothes. "Get undressed," I demanded as I yanked my t-shirt over my head and tossed it to the ground. Never losing her mischievous smile, she slowly inched her wet jeans down her long legs, taunting me with what she had hidden beneath them. I was beginning to lose my patience as I watched her fingers reach for the hem of her shirt, pulling it ever so slowly over her head.

"Allie…" I scolded. She quickly removed her bra and panties, tossing them to the side. Her eyes danced with desire as I looked appraisingly at her beautiful, naked body.

Goosebumps prickled across her flesh as the coolness of the rain flowed down her bare skin. She tilted her head back, exposing the curves of her neck, and I watched in fascination as the droplets of water glided down her full breasts.

Slowly, I moved my hand up and down her slick side, my fingers brushing against her breasts down to her hip. I pulled her closer as I let my tongue run over her soft lips, parting them slightly. She groaned in pleasure as my hand found its way between her legs. I parted her pussy with the tip of my finger, moving it up and down her wet clit.

She shifted her leg to the side as I thrust two fingers deep inside her.

"Still questioning how good I am with my hands, All-Star?"

Her eyes were full of expectation as they roamed down to my mouth. She licked her lips in anticipation and pressed her body harder against mine. When I reached her stomach, I dropped to my knees, settling between her legs. I slowly ran my tongue across her clit as I continued to fuck her with my fingers.

"Mine," I told her as her hands tangled into my hair, burying my head closer against her. As I tormented her with my tongue, she threw her head back and cried out in ecstasy.

"Kane! Oh God, I'm coming…. Don't stop!"

I wrapped my mouth around her clit, pressing firmly as I moved my fingers inside her. Her hips jolted against me as I tortured her with my mouth, her body clenching firmly around my fingers as she came. I slowly began to stand as I flicked my fingers inside her, her entire body tensing with her release. I removed my fingers and placed my hands on her hips as I turned her around to face the tree. She rested the palms of her hands against the wet bark as my throbbing cock pressed against her.

"You want me, baby? Riding on my bike got you all worked up, and you couldn't wait to feel me inside you again?" I asked, taunting her.

"Yes... please, Kane."

"You better hold on. I'm going to fuck you. Hard. I'm gonna give your body exactly what it needs," I told her as I unfastened my belt and tugged the wet denim down past my hips. I paused only long enough to put on a condom before my fingers dug into her and I slid my cock deep inside her. I held her hips, grinding them into mine as I pulled back and drove inside her again. She braced her hands against the tree as I fucked her with everything I had.

"Yes!" she whimpered as I drove into her harder with each and every thrust, our bodies slamming into each other. She felt so damn good wrapped around my cock. It was making it hard to restrain myself. My hand reached for her hair, pulling her head back towards me so I could kiss and suck along her neck. My rhythm increased as my need to climax began to overtake me. Her body began to spasm around me, signaling that she was about to lose all control. With my free hand, I reached down to her core, pressing firmly as I circled my fingers around her clit. She tilted her ass towards me, grinding harder against my cock as I continued to thrust forcefully into her. Her body began to tremble as her orgasm took hold, her muscles contracting around me and pulling me deeper. My growl echoed around us as my entire body tensed and I came inside her.

She leaned back, resting against my chest and turned her head to look at me. With a sexy smile she said, "That was amazing."

I laughed as I wrapped my arms around her waist and said, "We've got to get going, baby." We quickly put on our wet clothes and hopped back on my bike. The storm was still raging as we made our way to the clubhouse. In an effort to avoid the attention of my brothers, I went through the gate and headed to the back entrance. With trepidation, she followed me in through the back door. I took her hand and squeezed it reassuringly as I led her down the hallway to my room.

"Baby, you go take a hot shower, and I'll go get you some dry clothes. I'm sure one of the girls has something you can wear for tonight."

"Okay," she said. "Thanks."

By the time I got back to the room, she was already out of the shower. I gave her the clothes Cassidy had found for her and waited for her to get changed.

After she pulled her hair up into a messy

bun, she turned to me and said, "I guess I'm ready."

"You look great. Always do, baby," I told her as I took her hand and led her out to the bar. I could tell she was getting a little nervous, so I pulled her close to me, guiding her to the front door. The music was blaring, and most of the guys were already sitting around having a beer. I led Allie over to Cassidy and introduced her.

"Cass, this is Allie," I told her. "Mind grabbing us a beer?"

"Hey. It's nice to meet you, and thanks for the clothes," Allie told her.

"No problem. They look great on you," she said, smiling as she handed Allie a beer. She leaned over the counter, glancing over at the outfit she let her borrow and said, "Looks like we're about the same size."

It didn't take long for them to hit it off, and Allie no longer seemed nervous. Hell, she was actually enjoying herself. When I looked down at the other end of the bar, I noticed Cotton giving me a disapproving look.

"I'll be right back," I told Allie as I stood up and headed towards Cotton.

When I approached him, he said, "What the hell are you thinking bring her here, Kane? You're supposed to use her for intel... nothing more."

This wasn't the way I wanted this to play out.

I wanted to have the chance to discuss things with him first, but Tony had eliminated that option.

"She's under my protection. Things have changed. Tony has become an immediate threat."

"Her brother betrayed the club!" he snapped.

"She had nothing to do with that, and you know it!" I growled.

"It isn't right, Kane. She has no business being here."

"She's with me. I'm claiming her as mine….."

"You better be sure about this, brother," he said as he glared at me. I looked over to Allie at the other end of the bar. She was talking with Cassidy, and they were laughing at something Boozer had just said. It didn't surprise me. The girls were always giggling over something Boozer had said or done. He was what people might call a true southern gentleman, and the women around here didn't always know what to make of his proper manners and country sayings. I was pleased that Allie was enjoying herself. I hadn't been sure how she would fit in, but from the looks of it, she was doing just fine.

"No doubt in my mind, Cotton. She means something to me, and there's no way I'm letting her go."

He shook his head, but I could see that he respected my decision. He knew I wouldn't make a move like this unless I was certain. I'd never been a man that let a woman sway him in any way, and I wasn't about to start now.

"What do you think Tony is up to? There's got to be a reason he's looking for another twenty-five grand," he asked.

"I don't know, but I don't have a good feeling about it. I have no doubt that he's up to something... big."

"I made the contacts we discussed. Made sure the girl didn't get a loan."

"Thanks, Pres. I didn't want to see her get in any deeper than she already is," I told him.

"How are you going to make sure she doesn't get the money from somewhere else?" he asked.

"There is nowhere else for her to get it. She doesn't have any family, so she is out of options."

"What's your next move?" he questioned.

"When he contacts her again, I'll get him. I'm done messing around with this asshole."

"Make sure that you do. I'm counting on you, Kane. I want Tony six feet under," he told me as he finished off his beer. He motioned over to Cassidy and said, "Need another one, Red."

"Sure thing, darling."

Looking back over to me, he said, "If you're planning to claim her, you better act fast. The brothers are getting antsy." He motioned his head to several of the guys playing pool in the corner, and their eyes were all focused on Allie. Possessiveness bolted through me as I thought about them trying their hands at her. I jumped from my seat and headed straight for her. Our eyes met before I even came close, drawing her full attention to me.

"Is something wrong?" she asked as I stopped in front of her.

I didn't answer. I reached for her hand and pulled her close to me. My eyes were drawn to her full, round lips, fueling my need to kiss her. I needed her mouth on mine… to feel her perfect body pressed against me. It was like she read my mind as her hands reached for the back of my neck, pulling my mouth down to hers. Her lips ground into mine as the kiss became more urgent and filled with need. What had started out as my visible claim to Allie had quickly turned into something more. My dick was growing hard, and I had to fight the urge to throw her over my shoulder and carry her to my room. A slight moan escaped her lips as I thrust my hips into hers, and I was just about to lose the last of my restraint when she slowly began to pull back. She rested her hands on my chest, and then looked at me with a sexy smile on her face.

"Umm… I think they got the hint," she said with a smirk.

"Who?" My girl was clever. She knew exactly what I was up to, and I loved that she didn't resist me staking my claim.

"Your brothers… I think they got it," she giggled as she looked over in their direction.

"I don't do hints, Allie. They know that. If there was any question about who you belonged to, they all know now. You're mine… all of you," I told her as I rested my hands on her ass.

"Damn straight," she smirked.

"Just let me know if any of them give you any trouble."

"They'll be fine. Everyone has been really nice. I like it here," she told me.

"You're always full of surprises, All-Star," I told her as I kissed her one last time. "I'm going to go grab another beer." When I turned back to the bar, I saw Maverick sitting on the end stool drinking bourbon. I knew then that something was on his mind. He never drank hard liquor unless something was bothering him. I walked over to him, and he never even looked up as I sat down.

"I can't find her," he said just above a whisper. "I've checked with everyone that knows her."

"She'll turn up, Maverick. She always does."

"This time is different, and you know it. She stuck a fucking knife in my back, Kane," he said as he poured himself another drink. "Talked to her dad last night. He said that she came to him asking for money, too. You know… I can't help but think this is all my fault."

"What are you talking about, Maverick? None of this is your fault."

"I should've tried to help her. Made her go to rehab or something."

"You did help her, brother. All the time. She was just in too deep. There was nothing you could do," I tried to explain. "There's nothing you can do to help her now. You know that, right? She betrayed the club, and…."

"Don't… don't. I know," he said as he swallowed another shot of whiskey.

"What can I do?" I asked.

"Nothing to do, Kane. Not a damn thing." He was pouring himself another drink when Big Mike walked over to us.

"Just got a call from Nitro. Things just got real interesting, brother," he said as he sat down beside me.

"Tell me." Knowing that Nitro was our arms dealer, I knew it meant trouble.

"Seems Tony just made contact with him. He's trying to get his hands on a large shipment of weapons. Offered him seventy-five grand. Don't know all the details yet, but I don't have a good feeling, brother," Big Mike told me. "Serious, trouble."

## Chapter 11

# ALLIE

"SO HOW LONG you known Guardrail?" Dallas asked as she sat down at the bar next to me. Kane had explained earlier that she was Skidrow's Old Lady, and I was grateful that she had made it her mission to put me at ease tonight. She was easy to talk to, and I loved how her short blonde hair framed her round cheeks, enhancing her dark black eyeliner and bright blue eyeshadow. She wore a black leather mini-skirt that showed off her amazing figure. I might have been a little intimidated by her if I didn't like her so much. I can't remember I time where I laughed so much. The woman didn't have a filter and said exactly what was on her mind... with no reservations whatsoever.

"Not long I guess."

"He's an interesting one. Always seems so fucking intense," she said as she stirred her drink. "Like he's got the world resting on those shoulders of his."

"Yeah, intense is a good word for it."

"I bet he's great in the sack. All that pent up aggression…. Hell, I bet that man can do things…."

"You have no idea," I interrupted. "I love it, though. I actually love everything about him."

"Glad you two have hit it off. Guardrail's needed a good woman in his life. I'm glad he's finally found one that can keep up."

"I don't know about that. I'm still figuring everything out."

"Has he told you how things work around here?" she asked.

"What do you mean?"

"You know… the basics? Has he told you what it means to be a part of the club?" she asked with concern.

"He hasn't really said much. We haven't had much time to talk about things," I explained.

"There's stuff you need to know if you're going to be an old lady, Allie. Certain expectations that go along with being with one of the brothers."

"Such as?"

"He'll explain all of this to you at some point, but I'll tell you a few of the things I've learned. First, you never talk about the club… to anyone. Anything that goes down here stays within these walls. No fucking around."

"Okay."

"You don't ask questions. Just do as you are told."

"Really?" I didn't like the sound of that. I didn't like taking orders, and I had a habit of asking questions... lots of questions.

"Allie, I'm serious. Kane will make sure you know what you need to, otherwise consider it none of your business. You just have to remember that he will do whatever it takes to keep you safe. That's really all you need to know."

"Keep me safe from what?" I asked.

"See? That's the kind of question you don't ask."

"I don't know if I can do this, Dallas. This is freaking me out."

"Do you love him? Do you want a future with him?" she asked.

I thought for a moment and then said, "Yeah... I do."

"Then you can do it. Trust your man. Everything else will fall into place. The club is like a family. We look out for one another."

"That sounds really great, Dallas. It's one of the things I miss most... having a family. I still have my brother, but it's different with him," I told her. I loved the thought of having a family that would look out for me. I hadn't had that in a very long time.

"Well, now you'll have lots of brothers that

will have your back. It's one of the things I like most around here. They might not look like much, but these guys have heart. They are loyal, and they'll never let you down."

"Wow. You have no idea how great that sounds to me. What else? Are there more rules I need to know about?" I asked.

"There's always stuff going on around here. The guys work hard, and when they're done, they play hard. Keep your nose out of their business, and steer clear of the sweet butts."

"Sweet butts?" I asked. "What the hell is a sweet butt?"

"The club whores. Every club has them. A couple of the girls are okay, but the rest are nothing but trouble. They're always looking to get their claws into one of the brothers, but none of the guys around here wants a stretched out has-been for an old lady."

"You are too much, Dallas," I said, laughing.

"Truth, girl," she said with a wink. "No man wants someone's sloppy seconds."

I looked down at the other end of the bar and asked, "What about Cassidy? Is she one of them?" I really liked her, and I hated the thought of not being able to talk to her.

"She's different. Cassidy isn't like the others. She's more… selective." I didn't know what to think. I knew things were different here, but this was a little much.

"So all the guys have been with these girls? Even Kane?" I asked, feeling a little nauseous at the thought.

"Don't ask questions you already know the answer to, girl."

Arms slowly wrapped around my waist, and I felt the bristles of Kane's beard brush against my cheek. Just having him close made my doubts slip away. I didn't care about his past. I just cared about his future.

"You ready to get out of here?" he whispered in my ear.

"Whenever you are," I told him as I leaned back into his chest.

"Let's roll," he said as he nipped at my ear.

"You kids have fun," Dallas said playfully. "I know *you* will, Allie."

We both laughed, and I gave her a quick hug before I said, "Thank you, Dallas. I really had fun hanging out with you tonight."

## Chapter 12

# GUARDRAIL

M Y PHONE STARTED ringing early this morning, but I couldn't make myself answer it. There was only one thing that was going to get me to wake up… Allie. I wanted to feel her body pressed against mine, to hear her call out my name over and over while I fucked her senseless. I was pissed when I rolled over, though, and found that she wasn't in the bed with me. I lifted up on my elbows and quickly realized that her clothes were missing. Fuck! She had slipped out of the house without me noticing. When my phone started again with its incessant ringing, I thought it might be her. I reached over to the nightstand and answered it.

"Yeah," I grumbled.

"She's on the move," Big Mike announced. "Looks like she's heading back to her house."

"What the fuck?"

"She got another message from Tony about a

half an hour ago. He told her to meet him there. I've got two of the brothers on her, but you might want to get over there."

"Tell them not to lose sight of her. I'm on my way," I ordered.

Anger surged through me as I threw on my clothes. I tried to warn her that Tony was up to no good, but she wouldn't listen. She was just too damn stubborn. She was determined to help him, but there was no way for her to help someone like him. He was out for himself, and he didn't care who he brought down with him.

When I pulled up to Allie's house, Rico and Boozer were standing outside her living room window with their weapons drawn. They both watched as I pulled into the driveway. I didn't stop to ask what was going on. I just headed straight for the front door.

I stopped as I heard Tony shout, "I've seen you with him. I know what you've been doing, Allie! What the fuck were you thinking?"

"I don't know what you're talking about!" she yelled back.

"You've been to their clubhouse. You've been in his bed! I've been watching you, sis. I know you've sided with them."

"What the hell are you talking about? I've ALWAYS been on your side! He's just my contractor!"

"Are you so fucking stupid you don't even

know who you let crawl between your goddamn legs? Fuck, Allie. He's the Vice President of Satan's Fury. They've been after me for weeks, and now you're fucking the man that wants to put a bullet in my head!" Tony shouted.

"You're lying, Tony!" she screamed. "He'd never do anything like that!"

"You are so fucking stupid! Don't you know he just used you for a good fuck? How could you be so damn naïve? A man like him would never settle for woman like you, Allie. Surely you don't think this guy actually gives a fuck about you. You're just a piece of ass to him!"

"You're wrong, Tony," she said, not sounding very sure of herself. I could tell that she was beginning to have her doubts, and I didn't like it. Not one fucking bit.

"Just give me the money so I can get the hell out of here!"

"I don't have the money, Tony. They wouldn't give me the loan," she cried.

"Fuuckk!!" he shouted.

I heard something fall before Allie shouted, "Tony, what are you doing? I told you I don't have the money! Put the gun away!"

"You're fucking one of them, and now you're turning your back on me! You were supposed to stand by me! I'm your brother. The only family you've got left, and you tossed me to the side like a bag of garbage!"

"It's not like that, Tony! I've always been there for you. You know I'd do anything for you," she pleaded.

"You're a lying bitch! You're no better than the rest of them," he snarled. "Just another club whore that doesn't give a shit about anyone but yourself. And what for? You know he'll have his dick in another hole by the end of the day! You can count on that."

"Tony, please! Just listen to me."

I'd heard enough. I pulled my gun from its holster and eased the door open. Tony's back was to me, and he was pacing back and forth in the living room. Allie glanced over to me for a brief second, and I could see the relief in her eyes when she saw me standing there.

"What's the point? You've made your choice," he said as he lifted his hand and pointed the gun at her. "You always were full of shit. Thinking you were better than me, snubbing your nose at the life I chose. Look at you now… nothing but a two-bit whore."

"Tony," I said firmly. "Put the gun down."

He whipped around, now aiming his gun directly at me. "Well, look who's joined the party. I was wondering when you'd show up here. I'll have to give you credit, man. Never thought you'd fuck my sister just to get to me."

"Put… the gun… down," I demanded as I pointed my gun at him.

"Fuck you, Guardrail. I'm not doing shit," Tony snapped. "I know how you want this thing to end, but I'm not going out like that."

"It's over, Tony. Let Allie go."

"That's not going to happen," he said as he stepped closer to her. He placed the tip of his gun at her side and said, "Why do you even fucking care? We both know you were just using her to get to me. I should put a bullet in her right now just for the hell of it."

My heart twisted with his threat. I didn't want to believe that he would really hurt her, but I could see the desperation in his eyes. He'd do just about anything to get out of this. Panic filled Allie's face as she glanced over to me.

"What's the plan here, Tony? You kill her and then what?" I asked. "Doesn't seem like anything is going the way you planned. You didn't get the money you were after, so there's no chance you're going to get those weapons you were after... not that Nitro ever had plans to sell them to you anyway. So what exactly are you going to do now?"

"Fuck you."

"You're running out of time, Tony. The brothers are on their way here. Hell, they should be here any minute."

Tony pulled his gun away from Allie and directed it at me. For a brief moment, I looked over to her, urging her to move out of the way.

When she pulled away from him and started towards me, Tony pulled the trigger, shooting me in the chest. The blow caught me off guard, and I stumbled to the ground.

"Kane!" Allie cried as she rushed over to me. She dropped to her knees, and frantically tried to do what she could to stop the bleeding. I'd been shot enough to know that it wasn't as bad as it could've been. The bullet hit just below my shoulder blade, and I was fairly certain that it had gone completely through.

Tony's laughter filled the room as he looked down at me, his gun aimed straight at my head. With a smirk on his face he said, "You were right. I never had any intention of giving that money back to your fucking club. Hell, I'd have to be an idiot to give it back to you. We both know you'd have killed me either way. Now, I'm not going to give you that chance."

I felt Allie's hand reach over to my side as she carefully took the gun from my hand.

"Don't worry... I'm still going to get my money. Once I kill Allie, I'll use her life insurance," he said with an eerie laugh. He never even noticed that she was now pointing my gun at him. "Your little whore will give me my payout, one way or another."

"I loved you, Tony. I was always there when you needed me," Allie told him as she started to stand, still pointing the gun at her brother. "I tried to be the sister that you needed me to be, but I can't do it anymore. I can't let you keep hurting people… hurting me." Her hand trembled as she pulled the trigger and shot Tony in the center of his chest. Allie stood motionless as his limp body dropped to the floor.

## Chapter 13

# ALLIE

I COULDN'T GET the image of Tony's lifeless body out of my mind. The moment I pulled the trigger I knew he wasn't the brother I'd always thought he was. I'd lost my brother the day my parents had died in that crash. From that moment on, he'd changed forever, turning into someone I didn't even recognize. I'd allowed myself to believe that he was something he wasn't, a caring, loving brother who would always look out for me and love me... be my family. Ultimately, he was just a cold-hearted shadow of a man that didn't really even care about me, and it broke my heart.

When he shot Kane, something inside of me broke. When Kane's life was threatened, I realized how much he truly meant to me. The thought of losing him shook me to my core. Even with his deceit fresh in my mind, seeing him lying there fighting for his life made me understand that I'd love him no matter what. He was a risk, yet the most certain thing I had ever known.

As soon as the prospects saw Tony hit the floor, they jumped into action. In a matter of minutes, Kane was being rushed back to the clubhouse. On my way out the door, I glanced back and watched as the prospects removed Tony's body from my house and erased any sign that he had ever even been there. My heart ached for him, but my concern for Kane overshadowed all my other thoughts. I needed to know that he was going to be okay. The doctor that they had on call at the clubhouse spent almost an hour tending to Kane's gunshot wound. It felt like the longest hour of my life as I waited to find out if he was going to be alright.

When they finally called me back to see him, a sense of relief washed over me. As I walked into the room and saw him for the first time, I froze. A storm of emotion raged through me as I looked at him lying in that bed. His shoulder was completely bandaged and his arm was in a sling. He'd risked his life for mine, and I hated seeing him hurt.

"Come here, All-Star," he said as he patted the side of his bed.

I couldn't move. My mind still couldn't process the fact that he was there alive and actually talking to me.

"Allie…" he said firmly. "Come *here*."

Without saying a word, I walked over to him. I reached out and ran the palm of my hand across his cheek. He took my hand in his, pulling me closer to him.

"You okay?" he asked as his eyes searched my face.

"Shouldn't I be the one asking you that? You had me scared to death. Really…how do you feel?"

"Baby, I'm fine. Sit down," he told me as he gently squeezed my hand. As soon as I sat on the edge of the bed, he said, "You know, I've told you from the beginning, I'm not a good man. I've done bad things in my life…."

"Don't, Kane. We don't have to talk about this right now. You could've died tonight…" I began.

"No, Allie. Listen. When I started this with you, I was no different. You already know I was using you to get to your brother. What you don't know, is that every word I ever spoke to you, every kiss, every touch, was real for me. The moment we met, I knew you were it for me. For the first time in my life, I saw a future… a future I wanted with you. I'm sorry it started out as a lie, but you changed me, Allie. I love you, and I will spend my life showing you that every day."

Tears streamed down my face as his words sunk in and touched my heart. I could tell by the look on his face that he was being completely sincere and meant every word he'd just said. Kane meant the world to me, and I was relieved that he felt the same way.

"I love you too, Kane. I've never known love like this before. Thank you for being there for me, protecting me, and keeping me safe. You saved me in more ways than you know. I love my brother, and always will. He just wasn't the man that I thought he was. I hate what he did to you and your club, but his betrayal finally opened my eyes."

"No one would blame you for the way you felt about your brother. Of course you loved him. He was the only family you had. He didn't realize how lucky he was to have you. You were a good sister, Allie. You've gotta know that," he said as he ran his hands down my arms, comforting me. "You're mine now. I'm claiming you as my Old Lady, which means you've got a new family now. One that will be there whenever you need them. Loyal to the end."

"I never thought I'd have that again. I desperately wanted it, but it always seemed just out of my reach," I said, wiping the tears from my eyes. "I want this, Kane. I want you."

"You've got me," he said, pulling me over and pressing his lips against mine, sealing his promise with a kiss. When I leaned into him, deepening the kiss, he groaned in discomfort. In the passion of the moment, I'd forgotten about his wound and hurt him. I jumped back, saying, "I'm sorry, Kane! Are you okay?"

"Hush, Allie. I'm fine. Just lay with me for a little bit. I need to rest my eyes."

I curled up beside him, settling myself in the crook of his arm. I felt the tension from the day begin to drift from my body as I listened to the rhythm of his breathing slow. I finally succumbed to sleep as my body relaxed against his.

## Chapter 14

# GUARDRAIL

S EVERAL DAYS LATER, we held a short memorial service for Tony. It was nice, even if it was small. It was just the two of us, but I think it was better for her that way. I knew she needed to pay her respects to her brother, and what she was feeling was complicated. She wasn't really up for it, but I knew she would be glad she did it in the end. She needed closure before we could move on with our lives together.

It had been two months since that day, and I couldn't believe how much my life had changed in such a short time. Allie had sold her condo and moved in with me. I'd patched her in as my Old Lady, and she'd begun spending more time getting to know the club. They had quickly realized why I'd fallen in love with her and welcomed her into our family without reservation. She'd just started planning our wedding, and she couldn't have been more excited. I knew things were moving fast, but I wanted a family with her and I wasn't going to wait.

"Do you want chocolate cake? Or vanilla? Oooh oooh, or strawberry! Or red velvet? Oh wait! I know, I know, each tier could be a different flavor! Babe? Babe, are you listening to me?" she prodded as I pretended to focus on the football game. She was so cute when she got excited about this wedding shit, and I loved tormenting her. "Kane!"

"'Sup, baby?" I chuckled, never taking my eyes off the TV.

"Cake, Kane! We are talking about cake!" she shouted as a pillow collided with the side of my head. "What flavor cake do you want??"

"Woman…you're gonna pay for that," I said as I stood up slowly from the couch and tugged up the waistband of my jeans. "I'm gonna get that ass," I laughed as I darted toward her.

"Nononononono!" she screeched as she started to run away from me. "I'm sorry! I'm sorry! I just needed to know what flavor!" she giggled as she headed towards the stairs.

She looked back in time to see me grab my crotch and shout, "Oh, I'll show you what flavor!" Panicked laughter filled the room as I caught up with her and tossed her over my shoulder.

## The End

**For more Maverick, check out Ignite, Consumed, and Combust.**

**Ignite**

**Consumed**

**Combust**

For updates on my latest releases check out my Facebook page –

www.facebook.com/L.Wilderbooks

www.facebook.com/AuthorLeslieWilder

# Acknowledgments

I would like to thank Victoria Danann for including me in the Summer Fire Anthology. It was such an honor to be asked to join such an amazing group of authors, and you has done an amazing job making sure everything was handled. Thank you for all of your hard work.

I would like to thank Marci Ponce for putting her heart and soul into helping me with this book. I wouldn't have been able to do it without you. I am looking forward to working with you with Maverick's series. It's going to be a blast.

A special thanks to Brooke Asher for hanging in there one more time to see me through my book edits. You are a wonderful friend, and an amazing writer/editor. It's time to get your book out there! I'm not going to let it go until you do!! :)

A special thanks to my wonderful readers. Thank you for all of your amazing support and encouragement. I am working on Maverick's book now, and hope to have more information about its release soon.